Clint Faraday
57
Dead Still

"I was passing by on the road and saw them there by the rock. I watched a few seconds, but they were dead still.

"Well, I saw there was a Squirrel Cuckoo in that bush, so figured they were watching it. They spook easy.

"The cuckoo flew off, so I came down here after I called and they didn't answer.

"There they were! Like *that*!"

"Like *that*!" was a bullet in the head.

Contents

About the author

CD Moulton has traveled extensively over much of the world both in the music business, where he was a rock guitarist, songwriter and arranger and in an import/export business. He has been everything from a bar owner to auto salvage (junkyard) manager, longshoreman to high steel worker, orchid grower to landscaper, tropical fish farmer to commercial fisherman. He started writing books in 1983 and has published more than 350 books as of January 1, 2023. His most popular books to date are about research with orchids, though much of his science fiction and fantasy work has proven popular. He wrote the CD Grimes, PI series, and the Det. Nick Storie series, Clint Faraday series, and many other works.

He now resides in Gualaca, Chiriqui, Panamá, where he writes books, plays music with friends, does research with orchids and medicinal plants. He has lately become involved in fighting for the rights of the indigenous people, who are among his closest friends, and in fighting the extreme corruption in the courts and police in Panamá.

He offers the free e-book, *Fading Paradise*, that explains what he has been through because of the corruption.

CD is the discoverer of the Chadam Protocol for curing cancer.

Facebook page Ambrosia peruviana for cancer.

Emily Sands jogged up the curved road above the river and sighed at the quiet beauty of the area; Gualaca, Chiriqui, Panamá. She was just past the part of the river below the hydroelectric project where the locals – and a lot of non-locals – came to swim.

How she wished she could stay here for the rest of her life, but she was obligated to get back to Colorado in three more weeks.

Panamá is paradise!

You have to get used to the different culture. You have to accept that no matter how good the vast majority of the people in an area were there were some who were rotten to the core. That was simple reality.

She found Gualaca purely by accident. The bus from Changuinola to David had blown a tire and they would have to stay on the bus for more than an hour before a repair team could get there. It was already seven ten. She didn't care to spend most of the night on a crowded bus.

There was one restaurant in the area behind the bombas, where the bus was stopped. The food was local and good. She had a Balboa beer with it and asked about a hotel or hostal. She was told they had a couple of hostals, but they weren't much.

A woman who was waiting for her husband to bring the horse from the show across the road spoke a few words in English and said Emily could stay at her house. The daughter was away in Panamá City for university and they had the room.

That's the way the people in Gualaca are. Open and friendly. She took up the offer and got her bags from the bus. The husband came with a beautiful horse in a trailer and they went out about two miles to a little ranch just off the main road. It was clean and comfortable. She sat up much of the night talking with Jorge and Nilsa Arrends. The view from the back terrace was magnificent. She could look directly across to Volcan Barú, the famous dormant volcano.

It was very cool since soon after sunset. She made some solid friends and knew this was where she was destined to stay. She had been everywhere from Changuinola to Chiriqui Grande, from David to Puerto Armuelles, from Santiago to Chitre and much more. She loved it all, but this was a special place among special places.

In the morning she had gone into the tranquil, clean little town. She would be welcomed to stay with Nilsa and Jorge, but she was too private a person to remain content for long in someone's house – home. That was a home, not just a house.

She found a little house not very far from the central park, which was a surprise (the park), also. It was very nicely laid out and landscaped and had facilities for children, sadly missing in David. Most people greeted her warmly as she walked along the clean streets.

She was not used to a place this clean in Central America!

Emily walked every street in town and the close area over the next two weeks. She met a lot of people. There were three large "Chinas."

The local supermarkets and many smaller stores were owned and operated by Chinese almost exclusively. They were called "Chinas."

There was no bank, Western Union, or ATM. People went to David, forty five minutes on the bus for a dollar and a half, for most things. It was quiet, another thing unusual. It was a true joke that Panamanians like noise.

Here it was quiet for most of the time. The church in the center of town had loudspeakers in the tower that played fairly good religious music at a volume that distorted into noise at times, but that was only Saturday and Sunday and not late.

Emily was the only gringa who walked around the town and traded in the local stores much of the time. There was a gringo living over behind the internet place who was a botanist who roamed the mountains between Gualaca and Mali. He was more or less a permanent resident for the past year or so. He loved the place and didn't want to ever have to move again. He was in his late sixties as a guess. He spent six to ten or more hours a day tramping through the mountains.

Well, he wrote books. That would mean he had to spend some time in his house.

There were a few people who stayed for a month or so, but far too many were the type looking for a way to make some extra money. Money didn't impress the locals, who were living life the way they wanted, thank you!

Some visitors were nice enough, but they couldn't see the beauty of the place because of all those trees and rivers and mountains. That type.

Aimee and Harold Barnes were more that type. They were nice people with a fixation about money. It was partly because of the sad state of the USA economy.

Emily came originally because this country has the strongest economy in the Americas. She fell in love with Panamá and determined on her second trip to try to get out of business in the states and retire here. The Barnes were mainly here to wait for the USA economy to get better.

"Honey, the money people run the country and it isn't going to get better for a long time. Even the war-for-economic-stimulation doesn't work anymore, as George B. proved. The sword rattling going on today shows how those people are living in a silly fantasy. They're dinosaurs!

She jogged around the long bend and glanced to the river.

Psychic! She was just thinking about Aimee and Harry Barnes and there they were! Sitting beside a large bolder.

They didn't move. She was about to call, but remembered they liked to birdwatch. She could see a Squirrel Cuckoo not fifteen feet from them toward her in a bramble.

She waited until it flew off, then called, but the Barnes didn't move or answer. Their backs were toward her, but they could hear! She didn't think they would be snubbing her. Something was wrong!

She moved down and toward them from about sixty feet away. As she got an angle more in front she could see blood on their faces.

She almost screamed, "Aimee! Harry!" while running toward them.

"Oh, holy shit!"

Emily yanked out her cell phone and called the emergency line. She explained to the man who answered where she was and that there were two dead people, gringos, there. They had been murdered.

"Murdered? How have you determined such there?"

"A bullet hole between the eyes is a fairly certain indicator."

"I would be forced to agree. I'm trying to reach the ... I have the bomberos. They have an ambulance, but you need the police for ... ah!"

There was a moment's silence, then, "The police and an ambulance will be there in about ten minutes."

"I'll wait up by the road."

She climbed back to sit under a big umbrella-type tree with lacy foliage. The botanist guy came by and stopped to introduce himself as Dave and to say he had seen her around Gualaca. She told him what she'd found and he looked down to the Barnes. He took out a cell phone and made a fast call, then told her Clint was in Veladero. He would be there about as soon as the police.

"They said ten minutes. It's been eight. I doubt it!"

"Ten minutes here is forty."

She knew that was generally true, but this was the police?

It was twenty five minutes or so. The police came and she pointed down to the rock. The ambulance came and the attendants stood by the road to wait until the police checked over the scene. A car drove up and an older man in prime physical condition got out.

She recognized him! His picture was all over the TV lately with that political murder thing! Clint Faraday!

Dave went to talk with him, he went to talk with the police officer and they came over to her. Benito, the policeman, asked her exactly what had happened

"I was passing by on the road and saw them there by the rock. I watched a few seconds, but they were dead still.

"Well, I saw there was a Squirrel Cuckoo in that bush so figured they were watching it. They spook easy. The birds.

"The cuckoo flew off so I came down here after I called and they didn't answer.

"There they were! Like *that*!"

"Did you see anyone on the road within the past forty five minutes?" Clint asked.

"Other than a few cars passing, no. There are some people swimming at the rocks, but no one between there and here."

"You said you knew them?"

"To talk to. Aimee and Harold Barnes. They came to Gualaca about four or five days ago. They didn't want to stay in David. It's too loud and dirty. They were from Indiana."

"Do you know where they were staying?"

"Well, not really. I think on the other side of town. I met them at the China by the guardia and saw them a couple of times back near the information center and once across from the Encanto Bar.

"That seemed strange. Aimee stood out to the side and he went in to get two beers and they drank them outside.

"I guess they didn't understand these people. They would be welcome inside – which is even stranger when you think about it! Aimee told me these people are very amiable and that she felt safe anywhere here! The only other bar they even went near was La Estrella in back by that little tienda."

"I see. Maybe just a habit they brought from somewhere else. Did they say that they'd been anywhere else?"

"Well, Costa Rica. Not staying in San Juan though. Those expensive places on the coast. Harry did say they were robbed in a taxi in San Juan and that the police wouldn't even try to find the man. They had the number and said the driver's name was Roberto Sanderos. Harry read it on the license on the visor. Aimee said the police probably got a cut. Only about three hundred dollars, but they never carried more than twenty since then.

"Rancho Dulcero! That was where they stayed in Costa Rica!

"They were in Mexico earlier. Cancun and Acapulco. Managua. Bogota. Rio. They'd traveled some."

They talked a bit more, then Dave and Clint left. Benito said he would take her back to Gualaca, but she said that she was jogging and would just go on. He looked at her strangely. She said she ran a chain of health clinics in Colorado. Death wasn't something she was bothered by that much. She saw a lot of it, if it wasn't often from violence. Hanging around and moping wouldn't bring them back.

He shook his head and grinned. She returned the grin and waved, then headed on along the road.

She jogged ten kilometers per day, three days per

week. She had seven to go, so get at it!

Clint dropped Dave off before going to the Gualaca police station. Dave said he had a few questions about the Barnes, but that was Clint's field so he'd forego asking them.

"Like: what were they doing out here? They stayed in cities. Like: why stay in the sideroads here? Why drink in a bar in the middle of a residential section? Why only shop at the China that's not on the main road?"

"Yeah! Like: who or what the hell were they hiding from?"

"I'd say it found them."

"Reasonable assumption. Catch you later!"

Clint went on to the station. He had papers from the main headquarters that made it plain he was to be given every consideration to the point he was often to act as the superior officer in cases of violent death. He asked that all information about the Barnes be collected. He asked where they had stayed and was told it was a private residence they had rented.

Clint went to the restaurant and bar behind the bombas. The Barnes hadn't ever been there that anyone remembered.

They hadn't been in the Jardin El Pueblo on the main road or the other large bar less than two blocks from El Encanto. Charlie's. They'd walked by the two two blocks farther from the bomberos, but didn't go inside.

At El Encanto, Lisa, the waitress, said she had sent them to Leyda for a place to rent. They were strange. They wanted a place as far back as they could get.

Clint got the address and made a map of how to get there, then went back to the station. Benito was back so they went to the house.

Someone had beaten them to it. It was a mess.

Some children were playing stickball on the street. Clint asked if they saw anyone go in the house.

"Some truck. Some guy and a woman. Maybe an hour ago."

"What kind of truck?"

"White. With a black cattle rack."

"It had one of those pull things on front," a small Indio boy said seriously.

"Puller thing?"

"Like when you run in a ditch. You hook to a big tree and it pulls you back on the road."

"Oh. A winch. Thanks!" Clint bought them all a soda at the little tienda nearby.

They checked the house as well as they could, but didn't find anything. Clint noted that they had taken down all the pictures and had pulled all the drawers completely out.

"Yes. A picture or papers," Benito suggested. Clint nodded.

"They will be gone."

"There may be copies."

They soon headed back to the station.

Clint thought a little, then called the number Emily gave him.

"Emily? Clint here.

"Did a white truck with a black cattle rack and a winch on front pass you between the main road and where you found the Barnes?"

"Oh. Hi, Clint. Let me think. I didn't notice much before.

"No ... but there was ... at the swimming hole? Had a dent by the right rear tire? That one?

"It was sitting just before where you turn in. There was ... a man and a woman ... by the trees."

Clint gave a thumb up to Benito.

"What did they look like?"

"I couldn't tell you. I just noticed as I jogged past. Their backs were to me. Typical Latino, I'd say. Dark skin and hair. Not tall, though not short. She had a dark ... gray ... maybe ... yes, gray blouse and short blue dress. Denim? I don't know.

"He had on blue jeans and a white shirt. Red and black logo or whatever on the shirt.

"I have a good memory, but wasn't really

noticing things."

"Thanks. That may help a lot. It might not be a good idea for anyone to know you saw even that?"

"I'm as much as blind and am too stupid to notice anything at all! Gotcha!"

She rang off. Clint liked her.

They had a little to go on, but damned little. The truck and description fit a lot of the things running around the area.

Benito said they hadn't been carrying their passports, but he had a copy in his wallet of the ID page. He was running it.

They took the envelope with all the personal effects out and studied it carefully. She had a small notebook, more an address book size, in her pocket. It had a few names and telephone numbers and addresses.

Clint called the only Panamanian number. He had checked the numbers on her cell phone. The only one from Panamá was Harry's, which he had also checked.

Her phone rang.

What was going on? The number was for Bet on the list. There was an address. A P.O. box.

"Benito, I think that, just maybe, there's a copy of what they had. I think I know where to find it! It will be mailed to her."

"In the states?"

"No. Oh four two six. David."

"Benito! Call David! Have box two eight five four seven held! There's no key here so it's possible someone has hers. They would have to know the box number. They haven't had time to get to David to open that box!"

Benito grabbed the radio and made an urgent request that someone go to the post office and get the contents of that box! Fast!

He pointed to the door and he and Clint got a police cruiser, hit the lights and siren and headed for David.

Clint noted any white truck with a black rack they passed. No less than nine. It would help if they had a year or model.

As they pulled into David Benito got a radio call. Harold Barnes' passport number didn't exist.

That confirmed to Clint that he was running from something or someone.

Clint called Emily again. "Hi. Did the non-existent Harold Barnes say what business he was in?"

"Non-existent? So they were running from someone, huh?"

"I really do think so."

"He never said. He did mention something about cattle at one time. Something about not ever eating another steak after working with some company that ... chemicals in the grain? Hormones?

"I remember that because he started to say something about dangerous hormones one time. Aimee said, 'Do you know how to make a hormone? Don't pay her.' It changed the subject.

"Aimee was a private secretary for something or other. Some little company that was about to go bust of something. I don't know what he did. Some science thing. He mentioned ... Kelthane? That had been restricted? Is there something like that?"

"Yes. A miticide. Thanks. We can work backward. His passport didn't exist legally."

"The logo!"

"Logo?"

"He had a golf cap with a logo on it. It was for a farm supply distributor in Austin, Texas! I saw it once. Agro-Solutions? AgroInventions? Something on that order."

"That's the best lead to follow yet! Don't remember this conversation either."

"You bet!" They chatted a minute, then Clint called a friend in Texas, a cop. He would see what they could find. Send prints.

Benito heard that. He said they had those ready to go to the USA. A set would go to Clint's friend and another to Austin, Texas. Maybe they would find out who Aimee and Harold Barnes really were!

And what the hell was going on!

There wasn't much else to do today on that part so Clint and Benito went to the officer waiting at the post office. He had a manila envelope with a sheaf of thirty two pages.

"They're medical reports. It's too damned technical for me to read!" Benito complained.

"There's a smaller envelope inside," Clint replied. He pulled the envelop out and opened it.

To whom it may concern:

I am Henry Billings, traveling with my wife, Arlene. We are trying to escape people paid by AgroScienceGenes to shut us up.

The enclosed papers tell exactly what the testing of a product of that company is doing to unsuspecting people the entire world over. It's gruesome and disgusting! They don't want it known because they will be sued for billions! It must be stopped and those people must secure treatment before the symptoms develop!

I am an organic chemist who has conducted tests of GIHB3812 and have shown that this product is dangerous beyond belief. The four chief directors of the company, enclosed, have received this information from myself directly. They are perfectly well aware of what they are doing.

It was signed by him and Arlene

"It goes to motive, your honor!" Benito cried. "Animales! Animales desgustando!"

"You got that one right – if you don't mind insulting animals!" Clint shot back. "Here's the four directors we'll be going after. William P. Huntington, Frederick L. Sanders, Donald B. Winthrop, Alice L. Carter."

"Well, we have to see what those reports say. I imagine Dr. Quinteros will know. I can well assume it's something we do not wish to hear."

Clint nodded and got in the car. They were almost to Chiriqui when he took out his phone to ask Emily to meet them. She would be there.

"Miss Sands? I don't ... I see. She is involved in the medical field and may be one who will be adversely affected by the revelations of this information? One of those directors was named Sanders? Very like her name?"

"No. She can read the reports and tell us what we're up against."

"That would be nice to know."

They didn't speak much more on the way to Gualaca.

"Can you tell us what these are about?" Clint asked Emily.

She took the reports and studied them, then went back to compare certain of them.

"They're reports on the results of certain of the chemicals that are used in producing meat animals. They show that there are unacceptable traces of certain ones that are carried in the meat.

"I think there won't be ... let me look at some of the followup ... yes. If the meat is very thoroughly cooked it isn't likely there would be severe medical reactions. Pork is almost automatically cooked enough to ... but people like rare steaks and those would still be very dangerous to anyone sensitive ... they could cause genetic damage. It would be disallowed for use if there were a chance of pregnant or soon-to-be pregnant women getting ... like thalidomide. You remember that.

"Let me see. There were as many tests on male subjects who ... they could cause genetic damage to sperm with the same kind of results in the offspring! This is something that must definitely be prohibited!

"Great fucking humping Jehosaphat! It's already being used?! What kind of fucking *things* would allow that? This is terrible!

"Clint, I don't swear! You can guess what I feel right now!"

"Benito calls them animales. I agree."

"Animales? No animale would stoop this low! Why ... Clint, I would enjoy injecting anyone who would put this kind of thing on the market before testing with a few things with, say, formic acid as a carrier! My god!"

"We have to stop them! *Now*!" Benito cried. "Animales! Animales!"

"Don't elevate these sewer slime to animals! They're a hell of a fucking long way below animals!" Emily spat. "Clint, I have to get to the states! Today! I can cause this to come out! It has to stop! I can use the computer to send information to my base and they can have it on the news in minutes!"

Benito pointed to the computer on his desk and switched it to outside use on the net. Emily contacted a number through Skype and talked while she scanned all the papers and sent them to six different points.

"I was in contact with the centers that can get this information on the news. I'm assured that it will be on TV internationally within minutes.

CNN and others. These lists tell us the general area where the product is in use and all meats from those several areas will be quarantined immediately. We can be glad it's limited. One case is one too many. There are reports on eleven cases here. That means the shit's been in use for no less than ... eight months. Shit! Goddamned fucking sewer slime! I want those four *things* arrested and held for public stoning! I mean it! There isn't the possibility of an excuse for this!

"We're going to see a lot of deformities in children from the Austin area, minimum. If any of that meat was shipped it could get *very* bad, *very* fast!

"How can anyone sink this low?"

"Think of the *money* you can make!" Benito snarled. He turned on the TV and got CNN.

"... wish to warn anyone in these areas to not eat any meats other than fish and poultry until the extent of the agent is known.

"I repeat: *do not consume any meats* from the markets in Austin, Texas! There are reports that some of these products have been sold to a few markets in other areas. They will be traced.

"CNN demands that action be taken against those four persons indicated as directors of AgroScienceGenes who were, it has now been established on good authority, apprised of this problem eight months ago, but who refused any action because of fear of being sued.

"Well, you SOB's! You're about to get the piss sued out of you! I hope you're publicly executed!

"Sorry for my outburst. I feel this deeply. I have a pregnant niece in Austin, Texas!

"This just in: Dr. Henry Billings and his wife, Arlene, were murdered in cold blood by these people in Panamá, where they fled to try to escape these people. Dr. Billings is the one who, with his death, arranged for this situation to be known. Dr. Billings made the reports a full seven and a half months ago that were suppressed by these ... *things*. Reports of the horrible damage this product can bring to the yet unborn have been hidden by them for that time!

"This just in. Donald Winthrop and William Huntington have been arrested and charged with multiple heinous murders. There were no less than ... how many, Irene? Still births that have been directly tied to this product?"

A small voice from off-camera, "Thirty seven, proven."

"Frederick Sanders is in his private jet. We don't know where he is trying to go, but we are assured by most places he could reach that he will not be allowed, ever, to land under any circumstances, so if you aren't past the point of no return, you'd better take your chances here, Slimewad!

"Alice Carter, the last of the persons known to this point who infected the race with their unbelievable sordidity, is in hiding somewhere. A picture will shortly be shown. If anyone identifies her for arrest this station will give them a fifty thousand dollar reward!

"To repeat what this very special broadcast concerns, and I'm informed that I am carried on most major channels, is a crime that is too horrible to contemplate...."

"Well, the word is out, but that won't help the ones already affected," Emily said tiredly. "I agree totally with that man. This is a crime too horrible to even contemplate."

Her Skype circuit buzzed and she answered. "Em? John here. Sanders plane was shot down over the gulf. We don't know who did it. I'd like to have whoever declared Citizen of the World and a million dollars a year donated to them for life!"

"We have to find Alice Carter. You know how I am about most things, that I've gone so far as to let murderers escape so we wouldn't have to prosecute them, but I'm the opposite on this one. I want her found. I'll go anywhere, at anytime, to see her caught!" Clint said. "I also want it made clear to the world that the world they've allowed to be created made things like this inevitable. Those damned slimy money-manipulators have to be called to account ... god, I sound corny to myself! You know what I mean!"

"This means we have at least nine months of severely genetically damaged babies," Emily said. "Clint, find her! Give me thirty seconds alone with her when you do. Nothing can make up for what she's done, but I can make it damned plain to anyone else who would even consider this kind of thing that the price is a long way beyond what they can imagine.

"Clint, she won't come here. How will you find her?"

"I don't know, but I damned well intend to find her. Whatever it takes is whatever it takes. I *will* find her – if someone doesn't beat me to her!"

"She'll have millions to use to hide."

"I have millions to use to find her."

"Well, let's break this up for now and try to get some sleep," Benito suggested.

"Yeah! Right!" from Clint and Emily.

Clint left the station. Emily would stay there with the computer until she had done whatever was possible to do. Benito would use every resource the police had and was guaranteed cooperation from almost every country they contacted. It was noted to be released to the world which two countries made excuses not to hold Alice Carter for deportation if she was found inside their borders.

As soon as he knew he had complete freedom from being overheard he made a call to Manny Matthews, actually Marko Bocinni, a crime boss who had retired in Panamá to raise a family who would not be ashamed of how Pops made his. He was now a respected pillar of the community on Isla San Cristóbal. He then called Manolo, an agent for Interpol and others. Manny still ran the organization, which he had turned legitimate. He was powerful. He was a good bet to find Carter.

He called Judi Lum, his attractive next door neighbor in Bocas. She was a genius at getting information. Then he would use his own methods and methods that had worked in the past. He called Tyna, his wife, and talked with her and his two kids, Nito and Nicole, for more than an hour.

He went to his computer and started a trace search.

He was too tired. He couldn't think straight. He would try to get some sleep and would go all-out in the morning.

Clint talked to his wife, Tyna, for more than an hour. She said she would try to get Mathilde to locate Carter.

Mathilde is the medicine woman for the comarca in Cusapín. She wasn't used to locate people before, but she seemed to have some psychic powers about several other things. Clint wanted anything that may help.

Alice Carter had been in Austin, Texas. That wouldn't be the place to find her, but may be the place to start a search.

No. The place to start the search was right there. The computer.

Clint used Google, Yahoo! and others to try to trace the name. As she was a director of the Agro thing he was able to isolate her from the hundreds of other Alice Carters.

Alice Maebelle Stein was born in Louisiana and had moved to Los Angeles when she was ten. Her father had been a distributor of sugar products from Louisiana and was offered a job as regional supervisor. He had taken the family there. The mother had stayed less than two months and had filed for a divorce. She wanted to go back to Louisiana. She hated California.

She abandoned Alice to get the divorce.

The father had moved in with a woman he was having an affair with, which was the straw with the divorce. The woman was a talent agent who tried to get the father into the movies. He was handsome and photogenic, but didn't have much talent. Alice got a few bits as a child actor. She liked to dress up, but not act.

Alice was passed around her relatives for three years, then had run away to Louisiana where her mother was living with a man who owned a bar. He was a thug. He threw Alice out and the mother hadn't cared. She was an alcoholic. She died eleven months later – of AIDS. The man died less than a year after that.

Alice met a man, Brandon Carter, who ran a brokerage that handled a lot of agricultural stocks and futures. There was a marriage of convenience. She was more than presentable and knowledgeable about the field. She had a talent for making money. She had worked for quite a stint with a woman, Teresa Halwin, in a sort of cooperative with money people in a lot of projects. They stayed in touch.

After a year Alice had started traveling over all the Americas to make deals having to do with agricultural products. She invested heavily in genetic research and "Product enhancement procedures." She left Carter and moved in with William Huntington, owner of a livestock food supplies company and genetic research center. Huntington had financed several ventures that paid off. Big! So did a couple of the Halwin deals.

She had left Huntington less than a year ago and was living with a man from Jamaica. He was thought to be an enforcer type for a drug distributor.

Enforcer? That explained which drugs were meant!

Jamaica was one of the countries that would "Wait and see what charges were brought and how authentic those charges proved to be after intense investigation before deporting someone accused of something or other in the United States."

Clint thought for a few minutes, then called Benito, who said he had some information, but it didn't add anything he could see.

Manny called him. It seemed Alice Carter had strong connections in Costa Rica, where she had backed two former presidents and one unsuccessful runner. She had set up a deal with cattle production that was making her company a lot of money while hurting Costa Rica. That had to do with the Halwin woman.

"Clint, the Huntington character was put in an impossible situation. The others were there with their eyes wide open. He's just a dupe. Try to determine if he actually was informed about this. I don't think he was. The other three would keep it from him."

Clint agreed to see what he could do. Manny said he would send a top lawyer who could probably get him off, but he was a decent person who would never get out from under that cloud.

"Maybe we can work something out. If he's innocent, I'll do everything I can, but he's got to explain why he was there at all!"

Manny agreed with that.

"Clint, do you have any idea where I can bring a more directed search for her?"

"Jamaica. She's living with an enforcer from there."

"Name?"

"Liam LeFevre."

"Fifteen minutes!" He rang off. Clint called Manolo, who said there were reports about LeFevre and stolen art. He'd have his sources checked.

Clint smirked and called Benito. He said to have a ticket ready for him to go to Jamaica. Benito didn't question it. He said it would be there at any time.

He smirked again and sat back.

"Stop it, you fucking idiot! Every time you get smug you get slapped down!" he mumbled.

Manny called back. "They are very definitely not in Jamaica and aren't likely to go there. LeFevre's definitely persona non grata there. He wouldn't survive half an hour and knows it. Two groups have had a long and bitter dispute over territory. The one he was with lost, about a month ago. LeFevre had hit two big shots with the winner.

"Clint, try Nicaragua. There's a suspicious thing about a plane that went to Barbados to let two passengers off. They went directly to a boat. That boat is being watched. It's about three quarters of an hour off the Nicaraguan coast. Halwin may be in Nicaragua. I think I'll look into her."

"Thanks, Manny. She does have connections in the area. I agree about Halwin."

"So does LeFevre. His brother's married to a woman there. I can have all that information ready for you in a few minutes."

They chatted a bit. Clint called Manolo again. Manolo would check on family connections.

Clint looked in the little mirror over the desk. "See, fuckhead? Get smug, get smacked!"

He put everything he might need in a backpack and called Benito to say that the ticket wouldn't be for Jamaica. It would be for ... he stopped, thought, and finished, "Costa Rica. I'll take the bus. As Jim Hanrady."

"Jim Hanrady?"

"My cousin. I've used the disguise before. I think that, just maybe, someone else will be in disguise."

"She'd be a fool not to be!"

It was just past noon when he was waiting for the report about the boat to Nicaragua. The phone rang. It was Manny on a conference call from the states, a lawyer named Crawford and William Huntington. They exchanged a bit of information.

"Mr. Huntington, I don't have time for games. I'll lay it on the line. If you lie to me, be absolutely positive I'll never find out about it. The nature of this thing means I'd make anything the US or anywhere else be a preferable fate.

"Tell me exactly how it was worked and exactly what you knew – and when."

"Mr. Faraday, I had some suspicions that they were up to something, but I thought it was about hiding money, not about the products! I swear!

"I might have gone along with a bit of money manipulation. It's simple survival in today's world.

"I swear to all the gods that may be that I had no idea it could even approach anything like this! I would never countenance something that would hurt people! My grand plan was to produce more and cheaper food, not to produce poison!

"I swear! I didn't have a *hint* about anything like this horror! I would have exposed it in a heartbeat and the devil take the hindmost!"

"He telling the truth, Crawford?"

"Yes. I believe he is. I've had a thousand guilty clients. He doesn't fit that."

"Crawford wouldn't dare lie to me," Manny said.

"Okay. Crawford, Huntington. I wish to thank Bill for working with us to expose this thing. It is too bad that we couldn't get proof earlier, but the Billings had gone into hiding and we never received his report. They made certain that the report that Billings made was never received by Bill, here. They knew he wouldn't allow any such thing. It was far worse than we ever projected in our worst nightmares.

"Billings had a statement in his report to us that Bill's life was in danger if they ever learned he was working with us. I must have misplaced that slip, but we may find it here in the office.

"Off the record. Huntington, tell me what you can about her."

"I really know a lot less than I thought. She can be very convincing. She would admit that money was the important thing, but claimed there were limits. They used her to keep me believing that we were working for the good of all where we were ... and all that sugary crap. I sound obsequious, but I really felt that way.

"She could come across as Mother Teresa when it suited her. She could also be the damned vilest bitch you ever came across.

"The whole world, life, love – everything was based on price. Money was – still is – her god and her devil. It's all that matters in existence."

"I know the type. Do you have any idea where she'll go?"

"Only that it will be where her money counts most and where she can get more. She can disappear, you know. She's good at being in the background where you don't notice her."

"She'll be with LeFevre?"

"If it suits her. She said he's got the biggest prick she ever saw and she was keeping him for her own, but money could get in the way of that. I doubt she's capable of actually loving anyone

"Mr. Faraday, she was a child actor. She can dress up to where you can be looking straight at her and you won't recognize her. She speaks French and Spanish and German like a native. She, just as a joke, dressed up with a blond wig and pale makeup and went with me to a party where her ex-husband was. She talked to him with a strong German accent. Said her name was Gretta Hermann. He never knew it was her! He tried to get her to go to his apartment with him!"

"Well, disguises can be effective, physically. Her money fixation will identify her I suppose. We'll tell everyone to not pay a lot of attention to what she looks like."

"I hope you get her! I hope she gets the chair! I hope there's a partial power failure that makes her jump and jerk for hours!

"I wouldn't blink if she was behind the whole scheme."

"I'm beginning to think she was. Thanks."

"Thanks, Clint. I think Huntington's a good person. You pulled his reputation out of the toilet and made him a hero. Maybe he even deserves it!" Manny said.

"Yes. Thank you, Mr. Faraday," Crawford said. They rang off.

So. She liked disguises and felt she was good. Clint wished he had known her so she could see how another person could fool even friends with a disguise!

"Go ahead, you half-assed fucking idiot! Get smug again!"

Jim Hanrady chatted with the tourist from Sweden on the bus to Escondido, Costa Rica. There were no reports that anyone like Alice Carter was there, but Liam LeFevre wasn't that easy to disguise.

Helene Stoker was moderately pretty and a bit shy, but said she'd heard so much about Costa Rica that was bad, but also a lot that was good. She would never consider going to San Jose, but these higher class places were still alright.

"Where are you from, Mr. Hanrady?"

"Chattanooga, Tennessee. Been in Ecuador and Peru the last twelve years though. I was here ten years ago for a vacation. San Jose was alright back then. Costa Rica is going down the slide, I'm afraid. I wanted to see it once more before it gets totally into the Dumpster."

"Er? The Dumpster?"

"A garbage disposal company in the states. I still use the expression."

"Yes. I understand. I, also, sometimes use a common expression from home that no one understands where I am at.

"It is sad how so often a good place or thing turns bad. It is too often for the mistakes of politics. People will select a person who is a fanatic about a subject, thinking this or those problems will be solved, but they always get worse. Fanatics are not realistic.

"I'm sad to say that I think the problem here is female presidents. They have made it almost illegal to be male. It must lead to a failure of the economy from the dissatisfaction of the people. I believe that man and woman are equal, not that woman is superior or that man is superior. I do not think it is wise for a government to punish any single group because of the way the culture before was different."

"I don't think I quite understand?"

"The women presidents. The Latin culture, more than some, held the woman down. Now the woman holds the man down. Either is wrong. The man today is not responsible for how his grandfather acted! That is moronic, yet it is the way the laws are now structured here. Costa Rica will fail to arise. It is sad. It is a beautiful country and the most people are good people."

"I don't think you can blame the women presidents for the sharp increase in violent crime. That is the worst thing here."

"You are wrong. A man is inferior because he is

a man, like a woman used to be inferior because she was a woman.

"A woman has learned over the millennia how to act. Her mother taught her and life was not bad.

"The man had no one to teach him how to avoid what has happened so he reacts in the male way, which is to war. The man here is at war with his government. War is violence."

"I never thought of it that way."

The bus pulled into the station. There was an older woman there who looked very much like Helene. She was introduced as her mother. Her sister, who was almost a twin, soon came to join them. They chatted a few minutes, then Clint headed for the hotel where LeFevre was staying.

"Shit! I thought I had her!" Helene definitely was *not* Alice. Clint had spotted her at the station at Paso Canoa, remembered the part about her speaking German, and figured she was coming in that way to establish herself as Swede. Wasn't the way it was!

The hotel was above average. There were about fifty people staying there. LeFevre was easy enough to spot. He was a very large black with long hair and wore a lot of gold. He wore tight pants to show off his main asset here. It was vulgar to Clint, but he didn't care. LeFevre was his link to Carter. He was the bodybuilder type and he did have a very well-developed physique.

Clint sat in the lobby, then went out to the pool. Most of the people there were around the pool and the terrace bar. None of them seemed to be who he was looking for.

Clint shook his head. It was easy to see which were gringos! Fat, flabby and out of shape! It got worse and worse. To see a man or woman in a skimpy bathing suit with a gut hanging – you wanted to vomit!

A couple of the women seemed to realize that they would look ridiculous in a bathing suit and wore sun skirts or Mu-mus.

LeFevre came out in a bikini style suit. The tourists looked him over. The men seemed more nervous and kept sharp eyes on their wives. The women who were solo were being overly-obvious. LeFevre gave a sexy smile to them all. He was suddenly being brought lots of drinks.

Clint grinned. Ten women after him and not one he would give a second short glance under normal circumstances. "Part of the job."

Now they were making it plain that they were willing to pay for a little entertainment.

A woman came to sit next to Clint. She was a bit mousy and plump. She said she was there to try to lose some weight. She would spend the days tramping the trails and would carry only minimal food. She had done that before. As soon as she got back to Virginia she would put it back on.

LeFevre was by the bar. There were four women who suddenly needed a drink. It was almost comical.

"I'm Annette. I also might like a romp." She grinned at him and pointed to LeFevre.

"What?"

"The way they carry on over something like him. You would be the prize who I'd be after. You're not a toy to play with for one night. You wouldn't take whatever you can get, then go to another one before the night's over. You would also tell me to take a hike.

"Want to bet I can get him?"

"No. Why would you want him?"

"A conquest! All I have to do is send him a note. Watch."

She scribbled on a piece of paper and called a waiter over to tell him to give the message to the big black man. Take him whatever was the most expensive drink on the list. About five minutes later LeFevre came over to them.

"Annette?"

"Uh-huh. And you are?"

"Liam. Is this for real?" He handed her the note. She handed it to Clint.

$250 for an hour and $1,000 for the night – if

you live up to expectations.

"It's for real. I have more money than Midas and pay for the best. If it's not as good as advertised, I'll let everyone know it."

He grinned and studied her. "You're on!"

"See you later, love," she said to Clint. They headed for her cabina.

Clint shook his head. That was ... a little too contrived. Could Annette Calvert be Alice Carter? Had they tagged him that easy?

How could they? He'd never met either of them and they wouldn't know anything about him – unless someone told them?

No.

Then why the act?

A woman came over to ask, "How much? I know damned well she made him an offer he couldn't refuse!"

"Two fifty an hour, a thou all night."

"Stinking rich slutty bitch!" She stalked off. Another one came to do almost the same thing if with a bit more subtlety.

The third one said they would all know if he was as good as he looked! If she bought and kept him he was. Trouble was, no one else could have a little vacation thrill with him.

Clint grinned and went inside to order a very good dinner. It was expensive, but worth it. That wasn't always true.

It wasn't often true.

Not much else happened. He talked with a number of people. He was sure Carter wasn't one of them. The pictures and descriptions told him most couldn't be her. She hadn't been fat at all two weeks ago so couldn't have put on that much weight. The natives who could fit the description were easy to check out.

He called Tyna, used his computer a bit, and went to bed.

Clint went down to the dining room to find that it wasn't open until 7:30. He was always up at five. They did have coffee so he took a large mug to the terrace.

No one else was up yet. He decided to stroll around the place to see how it was laid out.

There was the main hotel, pool, tennis court and all the trimmings. There were six cabins where the wealthiest stayed. He saw Annette come from number four to go to the phone on the terrace bar counter. She made a call, talked for less than a minute, then went back.

Why use that phone? Everyone had a cell and there was a phone in the cabina.

She didn't walk right for some reason. She seemed rather clumsy.

Maybe she had too much to drink last night and had a hangover.

The jungle was close. He went to look over the orchids growing there, finding a number of the showy species he had in Panamá.

He returned when the kitchen was open to have a delicious omelet, then to sit on the terrace to watch as the other patrons came out.

A maid came out carrying a heavy sack she put in the garbage bin. She walked out the way Annette had walked to the phone, but walked normally when she went back.

Clint didn't smirk. This wasn't the time. He put two and two together and just might have come up with four. He was pretty sure Annette Calvert was Alice Carter.

The disguise he was using made him look a bit heavier than Clint Faraday. To only use padding for an extra twenty pounds would seem odd when people watched you for any reason. When you walked your step would be too light. When you sat the chair had to react, if it wasn't a solid one, like you were putting that extra weight on it.

Clint used lead weights in the padding to match the weight to the size. Annette had thought of that and was using some kind of weight. When she sat or walked it was weight she wasn't used to carrying. If she knew she was observed, she compensated. When she didn't think she was she seemed clumsy.

This was a guess. It wasn't enough to be sure. There had to be a way to check it out. If he was wrong, it could let the real Alice Carter get away.

He also had the point that he was carrying enough muscle to not make his arms seem too thin for the rest of him. Not true with her. Her arms seemed too thin. Her ankles weren't thick enough for the weight either.

It was all just within possibility. He needed some more evidence. She really did have the money to make it hard on anyone trying to find her, Alice Carter or Annette Calvert.

He got an idea and grinned to himself. He might just have an idea!

It was going to be hot today.

There was something else that might prove it.

No one had gone near that phone. She wasn't wearing gloves. He had clear tape and talcum powder in his pocket.

He went to act like he was making a call and lifted the prints from the phone, then went to his room. He put the prints away and made a small pack, then went back to the terrace.

Clint was sure if that was Alice Carter that she would stay exactly in the character she had invented. That meant she would go tramping through the jungle, at least far enough to where no one would be able to say she didn't.

It was just eleven when she came from the cabina with a small pack. She went to the kitchen to get cold water for her thermos and a small sandwich.

Clint went to be coming into the restaurant as she was leaving. He called a hearty good morning. He said he was going to walk the trail for a couple of hours himself. Did she want company?

She couldn't refuse. She said that would be perfect! She really didn't know the trail and it would be safer if someone was along to help her if she fell or anything.

"Your boyfriend won't mind?"

"He was as good in bed as I'd hoped. He's still asleep. He doesn't do the walking bit. He can hang around and make those other silly females hate me. I buy what I want. I've bought him for the next four days and nights. He knows that looking for a little on the side could mean he loses what he has. I really wouldn't care so long as he didn't overtire himself, but there are some things that make it stupid to take a chance when you don't have to.

"Isn't that silly? I have no idea who he was with two nights ago!"

Clint got a thermos of water and a couple of ham and cheese sandwiches and they started out. Annette was a very good conversationalist. They went slowly. Clint was interested in the plants and took a lot of pictures. She liked plants, more the anthurium and bromeliad types than orchids.

They stopped on a large boulder about 12:30 to eat their sandwiches. It was fairly cool at that altitude, but they were climbing. They sweat. The pattern of sweat on Annette's shirt and jeans told Clint where the padding was. This was Alice Carter. The prints from the phone would confirm it.

Clint wanted to shove her over the side when there was a drop of a hundred meters or so, but knew they had to know what else she was into, which other products she was backing were poisons.

She was into something else. This escape was obviously planned a long time ago.

The trail looped back to a lower trail a few

hundred meters from where they were. Clint said he wasn't in good enough shape to keep this up much longer. He would take a little longer each day, but he had about enough energy left to get back to the hotel.

He knew Annette was more than ready to go back, but she would stay in character. She said she would go on for another hour and a half, then go back. The trail was good and fairly safe.

Clint went down to the lower trail and waved at her as she went onward. As soon as she was out of sight he went back and followed her. Se sat under a tree in just a few minutes and took out her cell phone. He could hear as she told Liam that he would be back in about an hour. Keep an eye on him. There was something that wasn't right about some stranger wanting to hike the mountains with a plain fat woman.

He went back and managed to get to the hotel about the right time. He acted like he was exhausted and went directly to the shower. He went to the terrace bar for a tall vodka Collins with a lot of ice. He took it back to his room along with a small bucket of ice the bartender gave him.

The net was working very well through his satellite connection. He scanned the prints and sent them to Benito. He then contacted Manny, who said the lady had several projects going, but none where there could be anything like what they already found. She was financing LeFevre. She may be trying to set up her own drug distribution. She had the contacts in the states. Her reputation was that she was colder than zero absolute.

"Clint, if she tumbles, you're in a really bad spot. There's no evidence that she's ever killed anybody directly but she's very damned well capable!"

"She's suspicious. I'll lay low and act like I'm not interested in anything about her."

They chatted, then Clint called Tyna and talked for almost an hour. As soon as he rang off his phone buzzed. It was Benito.

"Clint? The prints aren't Alice Carter's. They are from some woman called Teresa Halwin. I do not know what connection there may be with the Carter woman."

"Oh, they're connected! Big time!"

"I wonder where Carter is now. This has gotten very strange all of a sudden."

They chatted. Emily was there and Clint told her about what he'd found so far.

After a few minutes he rang off and sat back to think about the new development. Had he been chasing the wrong shadow all along? Was Carter the jefe or the gofer?

What a stupid fucking goddamned mess!

He went down to dinner. Annette and Liam were at a table. She called him over.

"It was beautiful up there! I can't wait to get on the west trail tomorrow! You'll come along, I hope?"

He thought of Manny's warning. "I can't make it tomorrow. I've been on the computer all afternoon. I might have to go to Ecuador."

"Ecuador? I never asked what you do. I assumed you were retired and wandering around."

"Mostly, but I'm an engineer specializing in mining equipment. There's supposedly a lode of silver that's in a bad place for what they use there. They want to use mercury. I won't allow that on any of my projects.

"That's in the field, of course. The newer facilities make mercury extraction safe enough. It contaminates too much without the newer safeguards.

"I think perhaps I can use more of a nitric acid – aqua regia method, you know – setup there because there's a lot of natural neutralizer and plenty of recoverable copper. We can take a look at ... sorry. My field. I tend to chatter away when others couldn't care less."

"I have a friend or two in Ecuador. Maybe you know them? Oscar Delante and Raul Cano?" LeFevre asked, then got an almost shocked look on his face.

"I don't think I've ... Raul Cano? The cartel chief? You know those kind of people?"

"Those kind? I mean, cartel? All I know is that he's in transportation." He was suddenly nervous. He kept flashing quick glances at Annette.

"You didn't tell me you know anybody like that!" Annette said coldly.

"I just met them in a bar in Jamaica. I didn't know they were connected with anything like that!"

"Well, you have to be careful who you talk to in bars anymore. You never know," Clint said with a wave. "It may be some other Raul Cano. It's a common name in Colombia and Ecuador. And Peru.

"I sort of like it here. I wish I hadn't signed a contract, but what can you do?"

They chatted a bit longer, then Clint went to his room. He wasn't going to get any sleep. He didn't like the way Annette had watched him. At all! He couldn't figure why such a reaction to the name, Raul Cano.

He used the computer to contact Manolo, who would know more about that kind of thing than Manny.

"Cano? Producer. No big deal. Known."

"I don't know why she reacted like she did. I

don't know why LeFevre got so nervous after I came back about the name."

"Weird.

"Clint? What was the other name? You said he mentioned two?"

"Oscar Delante."

Manolo whistled. "She was worried that you noted that name. Very big in moving things and in laundering. Lots of art purchases that spiral up in value and he re-sells them for cash. A million here, ten million there. It adds up after awhile. Name's not well known. We know he has a source in the states, but can't find it. It's routed and re-routed several times."

"Maybe we stumbled onto the source?"

"It's bigtime, Clint. It's the bigtime of the big-time. It's dangerous information to have. If they even suspect, they have to shut you up! Get out of there! Now!"

"I can't get out of here until morning. I won't be in this room if there's any visitor.

"I'm too old for this shit, Manolo!"

"You got?"

"Yeah. Glock 40."

They talked for another minute, then Clint put the second hard drive in his comp and dropped the one he was using into his pocket. He went to the pool area and managed to get into a chat session with four of the tourist women. Annette came over to say she thought he was going to be bedding down for the night.

"I'm just too tired to sleep. Maybe a few shots and I'll be able to get some, but I'm wide-eyed at the moment!"

"I can't sleep, either. Mind if I join you?"

Clint waved to a chair. All four of the others had sour looks on their faces.

Clint had phenomenal peripheral vision and had seen her signal to Liam, who was in a doorway to the side. She sat while LeFevre went back into the hall.

Clint hoped he would just search his room and read the computer, which was set up to make it look like he was exactly what he said he was earlier. It had a permanent log-in at an e-mail site that had a number of messages to also back up that story.

It was an hour later and three of the original four women had drifted off. LeFevre came to ask Annette when she was coming to bed. He didn't have anything to do. She said she was always ready for bed – when sleep wasn't involved. They went toward the cabina.

"She's a phoney bitch!" Laura said with a grimace. "You men can't see through her like women can. She was just here to waste your time and to show the rest of us she could get what she wants.”

“She couldn’t get me!” Clint returned. “I’ve seen the type before. I could see she was just showing everyone who’s the Queen of the May. That type turns me off!”

“Oh? What type turns you on?” with a leer.

“My wife. Period. I don’t believe in messing around. It leads to heartaches too many times.”

She grinned. “Shit! Foiled again!”

He laughed and said he was going to get some sleep. Annette and Liam had gone into the cabina. He could hope that “I don’t have anything to do!” was the signal that he didn’t have anything in his room to indicate he was anything but a mining engineer.

He really wouldn’t get any sleep, but he didn’t require very much. He was taking the warnings to heart and was getting the hell out of there as soon as he could get a ride to the airport.

But! Where in hell was Carter? Was he really after her anymore?

Clint was up and ready at five. He was lucky in that the truck that delivered vegetables came at five and he got a ride to the airport for the same as he'd pay a taxi. If the lovely Annette was planning anything deadly she was in for a surprise.

Not far from the hotel LeFevre was walking slowly toward town. He had a towel across his shoulder and was carrying a pistol.

"Don't stop!" Clint demanded. He slid down in the seat.

"I would not stop! He is a ladrone who would rob us! He would kill us for a dollar!

"He will not try to stop a truck. He will stop the taxi. He will have a deal with the driver that he gets part of the money."

So. That was the plan. He would be taking a taxi out, it would be stopped for a robbery, the poor victim would be shot. It's all too commonplace in Costa Rica anymore.

She had evidence that he was nothing more nor less than a mining engineer on vacation, but was setting it up for him to be killed because he heard a name that, evidently, he wouldn't even remember.

Alice Carter was dead. If there was anyone who knew too much it was her!

Clint used his special papers to get the flight that was already on the runway to wait for him to board. It was to Cartagena, but he could get back to Panamá easily from there.

Because of the way he'd left Costa Rica Teresa would know he knew something. Would she try to get him?

Probably.

Did he have anything that would stick? Could they even touch her?

No. A phony name while traveling? A lot of people do that. Fifty buck fine.

Was there any other link he could use to find where Alice Carter's body was? If he found it, would there be any way to tie it to her?

There was a link! LeFevre! His life wouldn't be worth a centavo Costa Rican if she thought he was the only one who could tie her to anything.

He had an idea. He'd gotten LeFevre's cell phone number at the hotel. He called it. LeFevre answered.

"What?"

"Jim Hanrady here. From the hotel. I'm already gone, but think the reason I'm gone means a lot to you.

"I was going back to my room later after we left the bar. Annette was outside your cabina talking on her phone to someone she called Raul. She sounded sacred to death!

"I really shouldn't eavesdrop, but it was so strange! She was talking about killing me! She said she already had a plan that couldn't fail!

"I know a way to get out of there. A friend. He picked me up and I'm not even in Costa Rica now.

"You are to kill me. I left because of that. What I heard next is important to you. It's about you being taken care of as soon as you report that I'm no longer a threat – because you *are* a threat!

"I thought I'd just let her knock you off. You were supposed to knock me off.

"I couldn't do that. It would mean she gets away with it. I thought you should be warned so you can escape before she can kill you. The ball's in your court!"

"What? Ball? Court?"

"An expression. It means you have to do something or she'll kill you."

"But ... I know she would. She wouldn't even think about it after. She can find me anywhere! I don't know what to do!"

"How was she going to work it?

"You catch a local taxi to the airport. It gets stopped by a street thug. You resist. You get shot."

"The taxi driver in on it?"

"Yeah. She has something on him."

"Well, I won't be using the taxi. I didn't show up. You found out I had already gone into Vista Verde and went there. I'm not in the country anymore.

"What if you can make a deal with the taxi driver yourself? Get her off your back and his at the same time?"

"So he brings her and stops where he was supposed to stop with you. Everything is what she planned except it ain't you in the taxi."

"If you can get her to come to Vista Verde in that taxi, how could it fail? The driver can't identify some big black dude with a shirt or something over his face."

"A towel. Yeah! It's her or me anyhow. I got nothing to lose."

"Well, my flight to Quito's ready to board. Good luck!" He rang off.

Now to get back to Gualaca.

Clint got off the bus at the parque and walked to the guardia. Emily and Benito were there, waiting. He called Tyna to tell her he would be home in a day. Two, at most. He then told them what had happened, leaving out the call to LeFevre about the supposed plot to kill him. Clint didn't doubt what he told LeFevre was exactly what was set up. This one he wouldn't let his stupid conscience bother him for a tenth second!

"Well, Austin, Texas, just reported that they found a body that could be Alice Carter in a burned barn. They are doing a DNA chart to prove or disprove it," Benito said. "So your trip was wasted for that. You did find this other woman who was probably the brains behind all of it. It's too bad you can't find a way to prosecute her for anything. She is the kind I would walk up to and put a bullet between her eyes the way she had done to the Barnes!"

"We agree with that!" Emily said. "If I ever find her, I'll probably do something like that!"

"We can just wait and hope something will happen to make her face prosecution," Benito said. "I have the police in Costa Rica keeping an eye on her. They don't know what for. I told them it was a crime elsewhere. All I want to know is when she leaves and what happens of note concerning her."

They discussed it awhile. They were about to go to their own places when the police line paged Benito. It was Costa Rica. Benito put it on speaker and said, "Benito here. What's happening?"

"I'm afraid we have very bad news for you,

Benito. The Calvert woman we were observing has met with an accident. She is dead.”

“Accident?”

“Not actually. She was in a taxi that was stopped by a robber. She tried to fight him and he shot her. We try to warn people that their life is worth more than their money. Money can be replaced. Life cannot.”

“Do you have the robber?” Clint asked.

“No. The driver of the taxi said he was a very big black man with a towel over his head.

“Calvert was staying at the hotel with such a man, but he is there and has not left since yesterday morning. He returned after only an hour and has been in their cabina since. We have no clue as to who the robber might have been. It is not the first robbery along that part of the careterra committed by a big black man.”

There were a few more details, but nothing new to Clint. They finally hung up.

“Well! That was what he called bad news?” Emily said.

“It was very good bad news,” Benito replied.

Clint dove into the river where the family bathed near Quebrada Tula on the Comarca Ngobe Bugle. The water was cool, but he was used to it and liked it. Tyna came carrying towels and his cell phone. She said a man called Benito wanted him to call.

He dried a bit and called. "What's up?"

"Hello, Clint. Emily is here and about to go back to the states. She has purchased a very nice little three hectare finca up just past the proyecto. She wanted to say hasta la vista and to tell you something she learned from your friend in Bocas, Judi.

"I wanted to learn how things are going for you. Dave is back and complains that he is too old to be in the jungles, but we all know he'll be back as soon as he finishes the book he's writing."

"How are things, Clint? This is paradise. I may have an offer for the businesses and can come here permanently!" Emily put in.

"Things are better than they have any right to be. Dave isn't the only one who's getting too old for what he's doing.

"What about Judi?"

"She's an amazing woman. I was in Bocas for two days and went to call, seeing as you had introduced us in a way on the phone.

"We were talking about the case. Mine. She hadn't heard much about it.

"I told her about LeFevre. She said a friend stayed with him a night last week and she told him she knew a little about the woman who was killed. You had told us a little.

"Anyhow, he said he thought maybe it was a drug dealer she knew too much about. She told him once that she was blackmailing the man, Colombian or Peruvian or something. She could get anything she wanted, no questions asked. He said he went through her things after she was killed and could guarantee there was nothing about any drug dealer in her stuff, that it was all bluff. Maybe the guy found out and had her killed.

"What do you think?"

"I think I don't give a shit to be honest about it. That whole bunch can kill each other off and I won't be able to find clue number one!

"I agree that Judi is an amazing woman. Here she gets information about a case she didn't know about at the time!

"It answers one big question. Maybe LeFevre wanted my cousin to get the word. She was blackmailing Delante.

"You're going back home?"

"No way! This is home now! I'm going back north because I can't get out of it!"

"There's no place like home," Benito said.

"True. There's no place like home."

C. D. Moulton's works are available on most major outlets as printed or e-books. CD writes the CD Grimes, PI, mysteries, the Det. Lt. Nick Storie mysteries, the Clint Faraday mysteries, the Flight of the Maita science fiction series, books on orchid culture and many others of many types. Mystery, adventure, intrigue, science fiction, humor, fantasy, paranormal, mild erotica, and factual.

www.ingramcontent.com/pod-product-compliance
Lightning Source LLC
Chambersburg PA
CBHW072205150726
48002CB00014B/1417